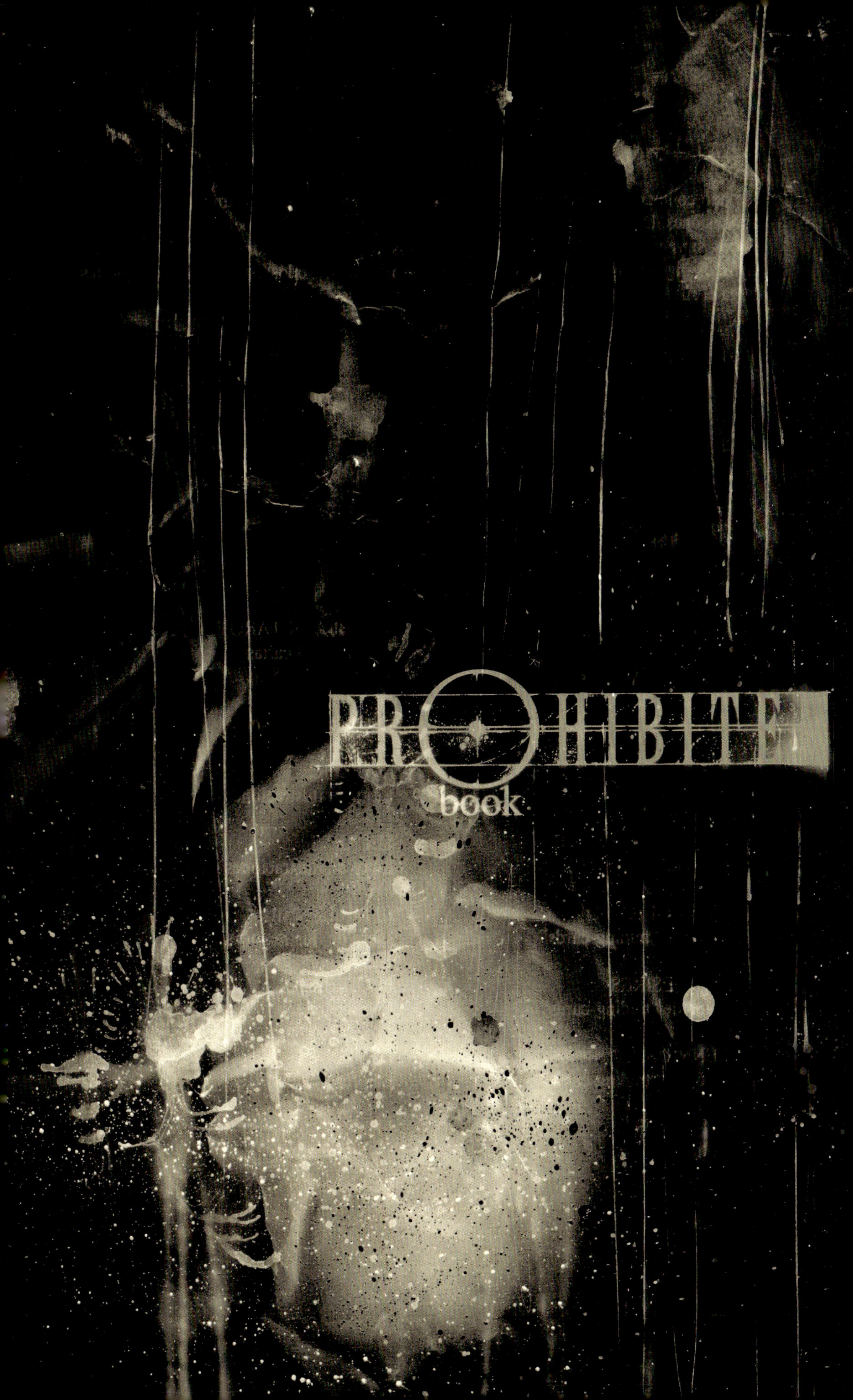
PROHIBITE
book

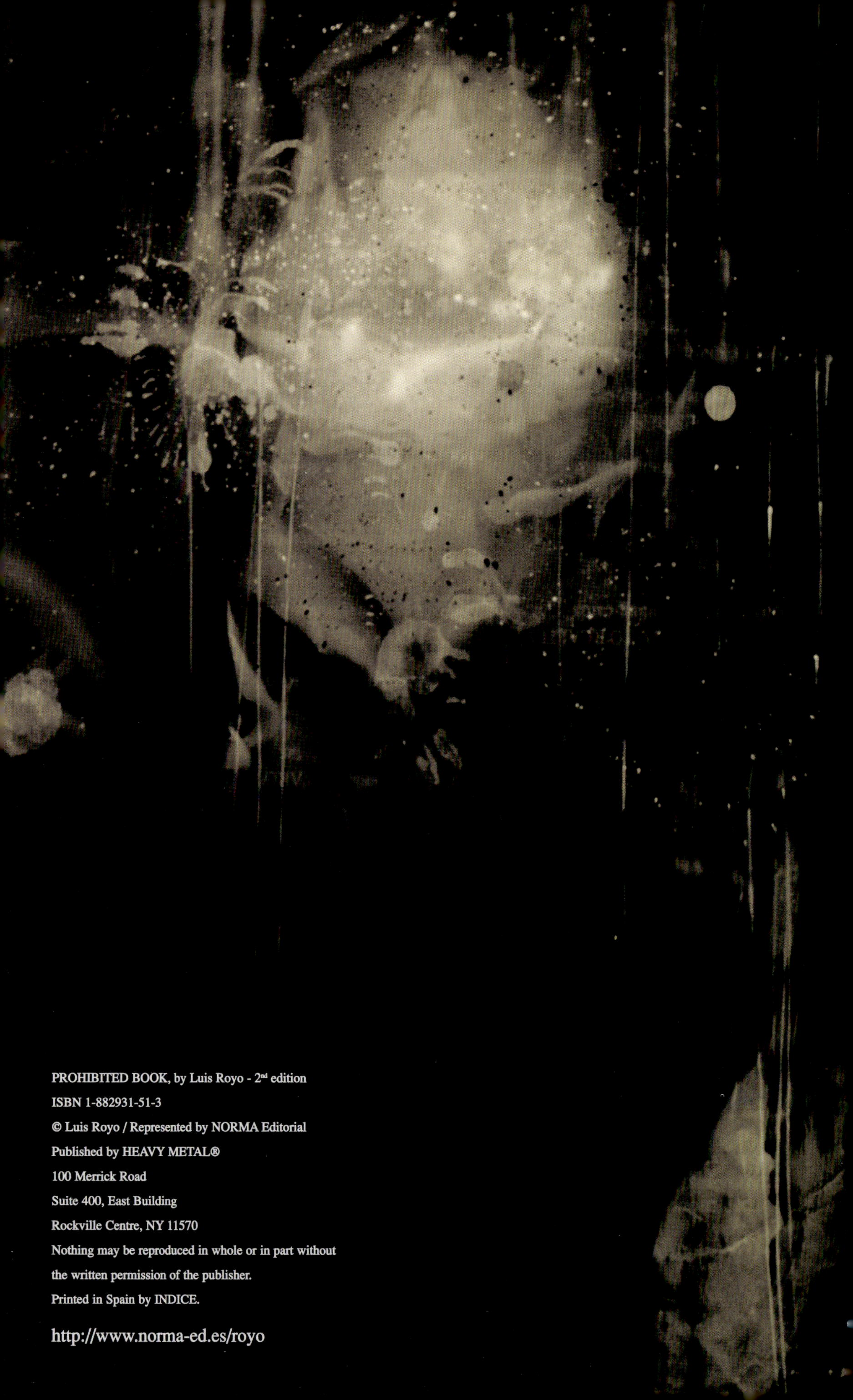

PROHIBITED BOOK, by Luis Royo - 2nd edition

ISBN 1-882931-51-3

Published by HEAVY METAL®

100 Merrick Road

Suite 400, East Building

Rockville Centre, NY 11570

Printed in Spain by INDICE.

http://www.norma-ed.es/royo

LUIS ROYO

Design and pictures by Rómulo Royo

HEAVY METAL

INTRODUCTION TO BOOK

Let's leave aside creativity, moulding, colour and so on.

These first words are to give us guidance to the form and attitude we should adopt when we browse through this book.

But let's get to the point, forget the old truism about eroticism, about pornography. Let's look for a quiet place, a comfortable and soft place to sit, even if it also serves as a bed with creased sheets. Let's take the book and rest it on the arm of the chair or on the pillow, and let's turn the pages with our left hand.

Let's take off our tight and uncomfortable clothing and put on a comfortable shirt or pajamas. After, let's slip the fingers of our right hand over our lips that previously had been moistened by our tongue, then let's move down, massaging ever so lightly to one side and then the other side of the neck, let's continue by moving our open hand over our chest, let's create some playful moments around the bellybutton, going inside it ever so slightly.

With the index finger, or perhaps with the forefinger and the heart, stretch while the rest of the fingers remain relaxed or make a beautiful "O" with them all, depending on whether you are of the feminine or masculine sex, let's bring ourselves to the inner surface of our thigh, with all the desire of staying moist.

From this simple and rewarding operation we're able to begin using our left hand to turn the pages, keeping in mind that the right hand doesn't forget its duty and continues with the gentle movements it knows. I hope that when this book reaches the end, the hand is left impregnated with the sacred liquids of our interior and that the pages have been left unscathed (and the need for a second glance).

The author would be satisfied if all the steps of this book work out well.

Luis Royo

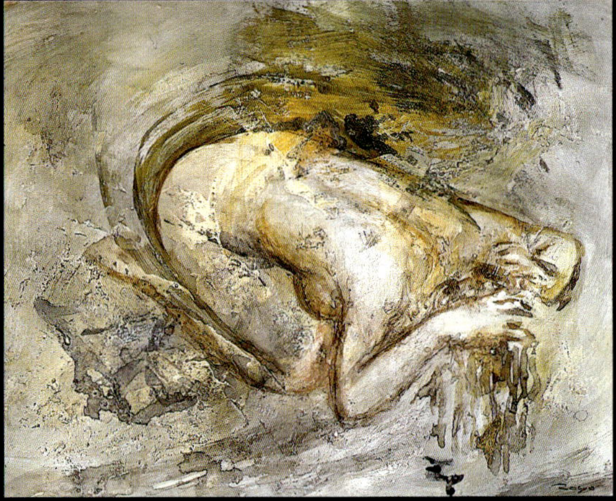

The bath

ACT I: THE PEACOCK'S TAIL

The first act, the warm water awakens the body, leaving traces of the dust that blocks the sense of touch, drop by drop it leaves the skin protected, it shines like the torch of a lighthouse does for the navigators.

Next, the skin is covered up, to create the crown of the peacock, it is covered in cobwebs that with open-work and embroidery play to cover up and reveal, centimeter by centimeter.

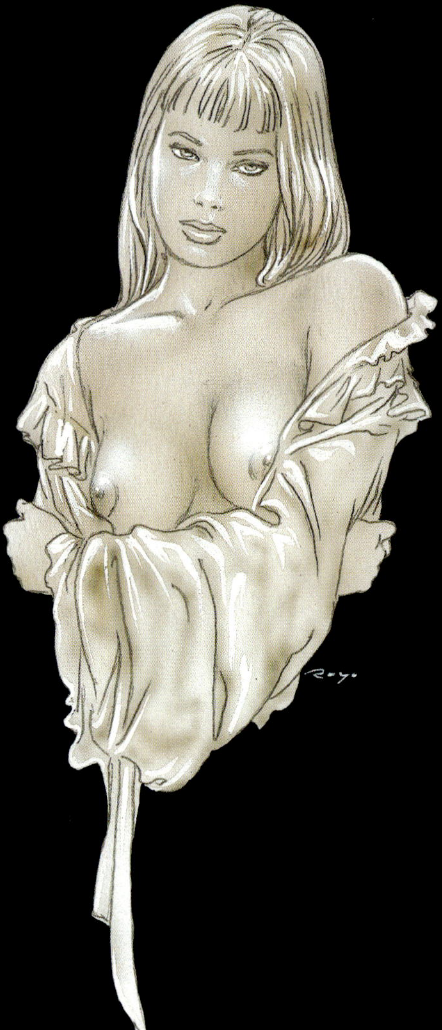

Provocative folds - 1995 (25x39 cm.)

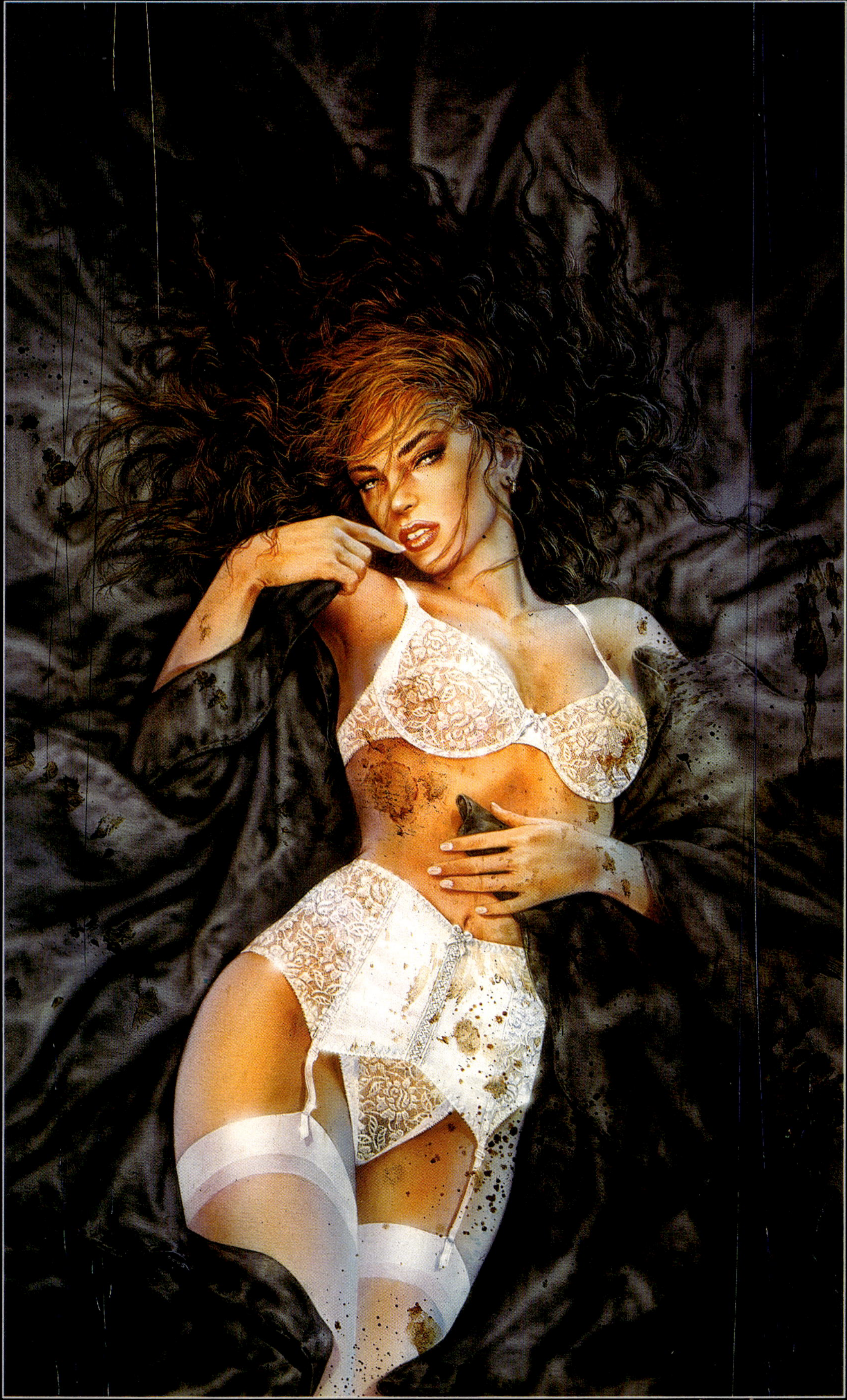

Meditation - 1999 (9x14 cm.)
Rómulo Royo

Slowly developing, like when baking a cake. The nervous system is running through the body and sending small insignificant orders. Move a leg and balance on one side of the hip, breaking the symmetry of the body. Give a direct glance and shift to the corner of the eye, while keeping the eyelids semi-closed. Take a finger and sink it into the mouth, passing very slowly across the lips...

Tick-tock... A bit longer 1999 (34x52 cm.)

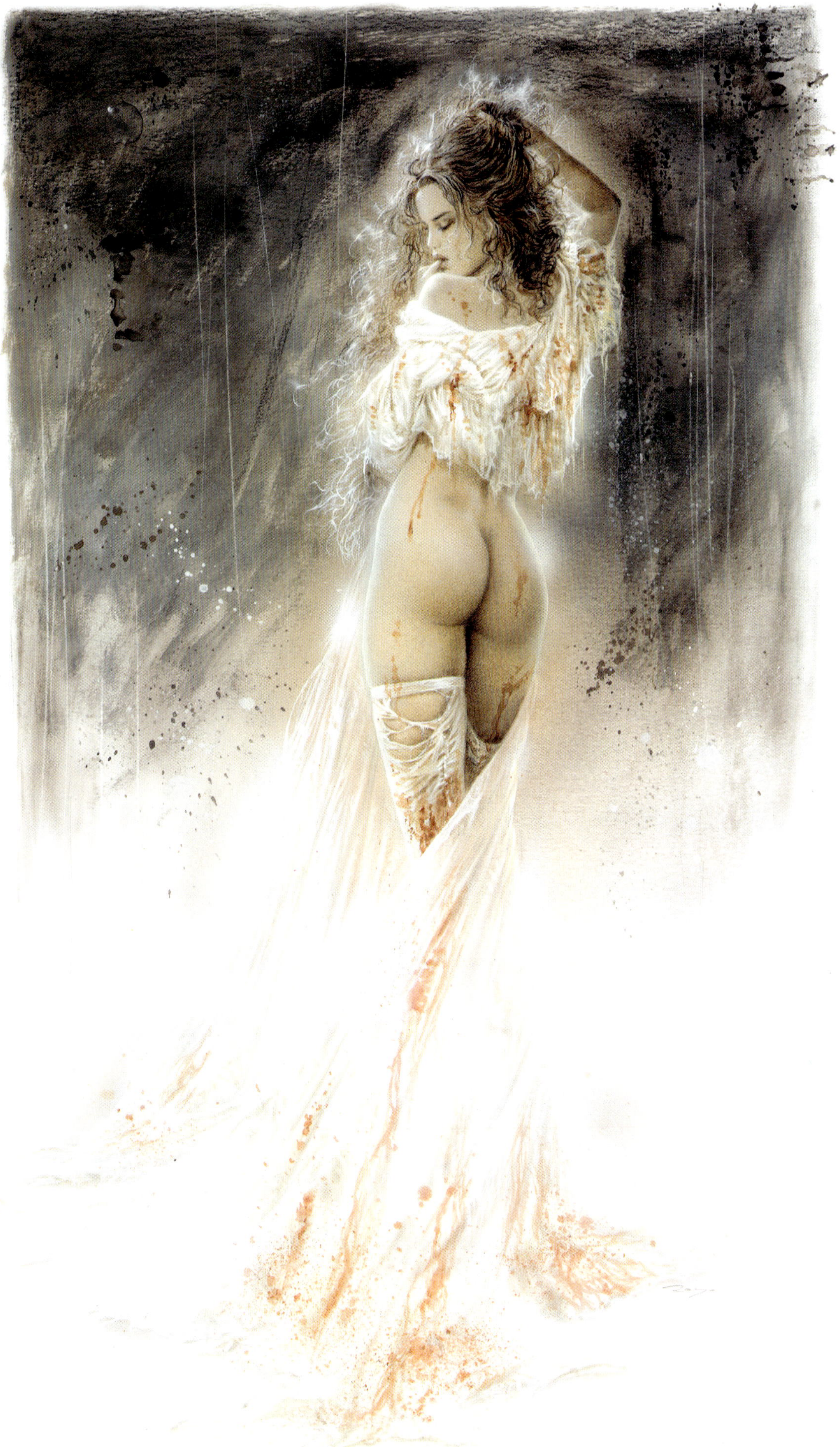

Little by little, like the bridge of a castle that creaks when risen, although in this case the sound of the creases of the clothes is almost imperceptible, they open our eyes to what will be our north, our religion, our insanity.

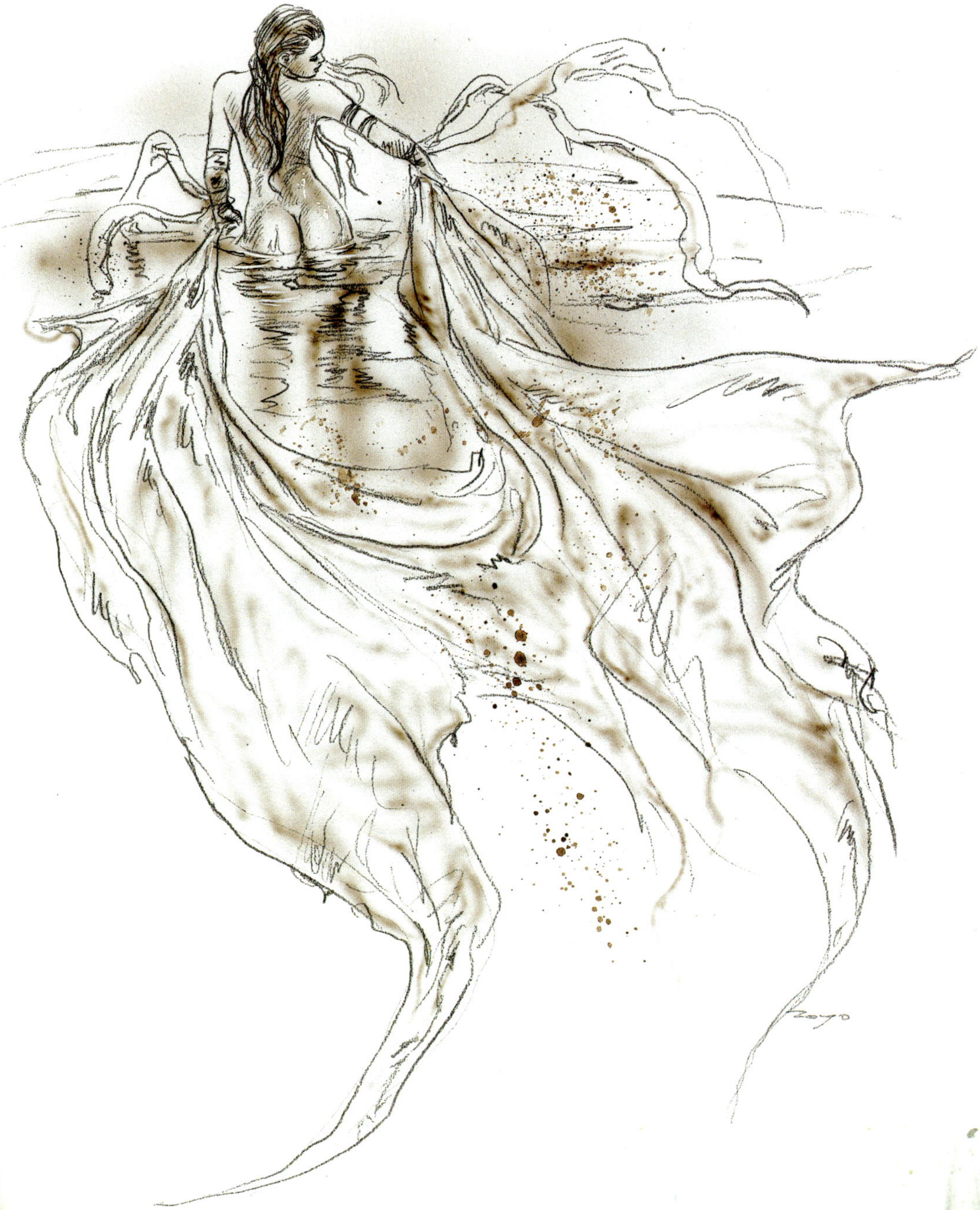

Prohibited II - 1999 (34x57 cm.)

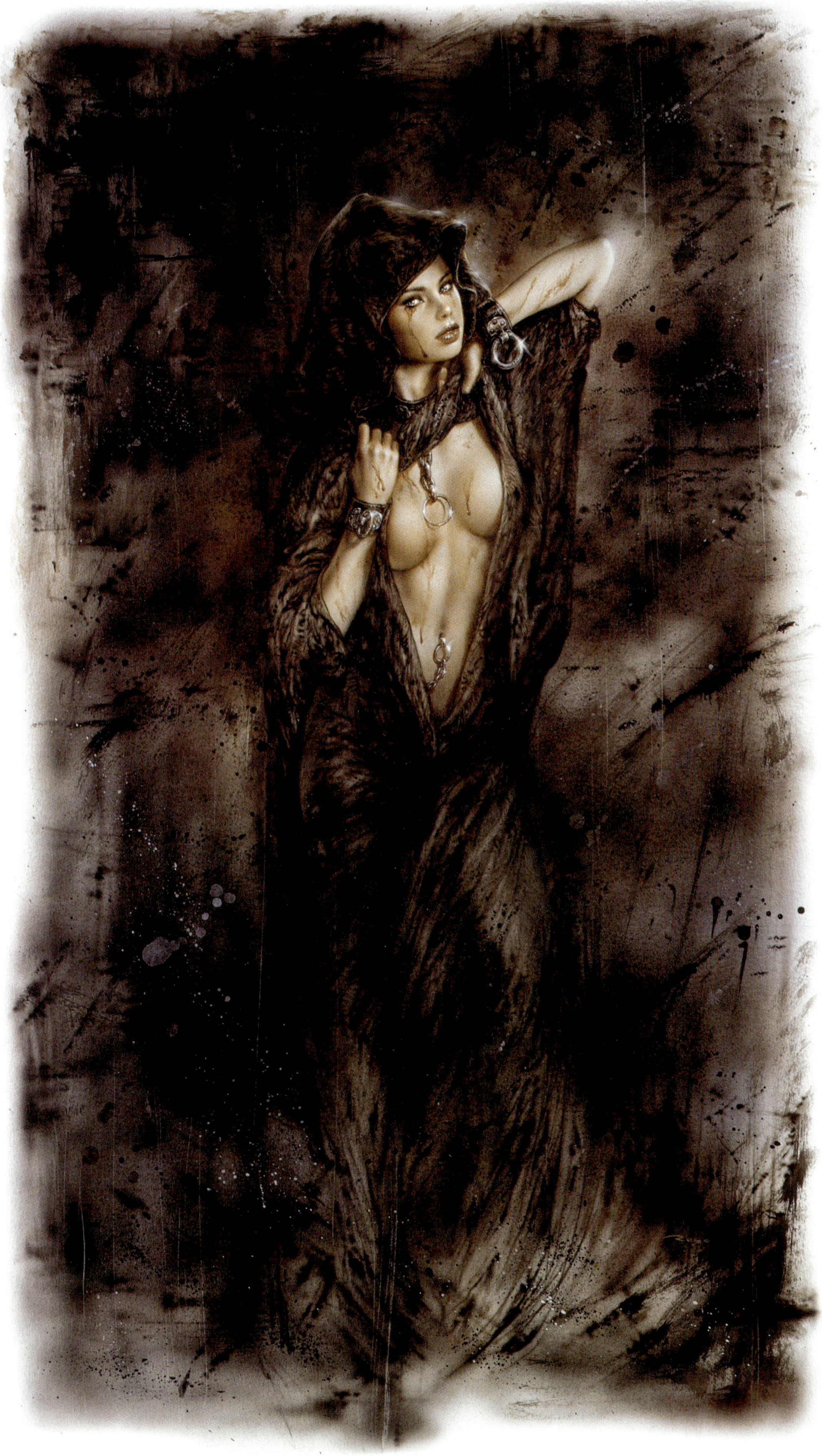

Clepsydra - 1999 (12x20 cm.)
Rómulo Royo

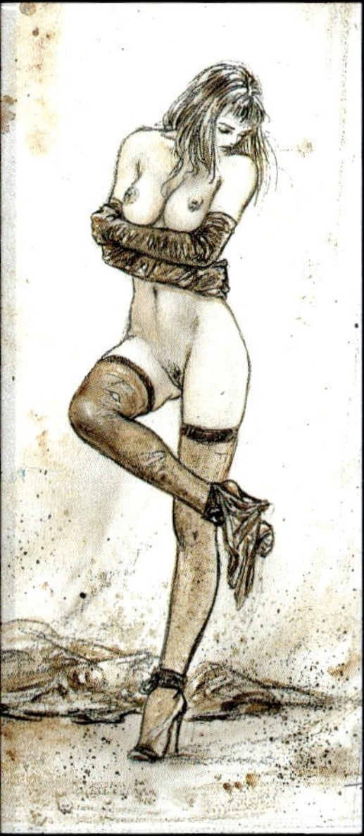

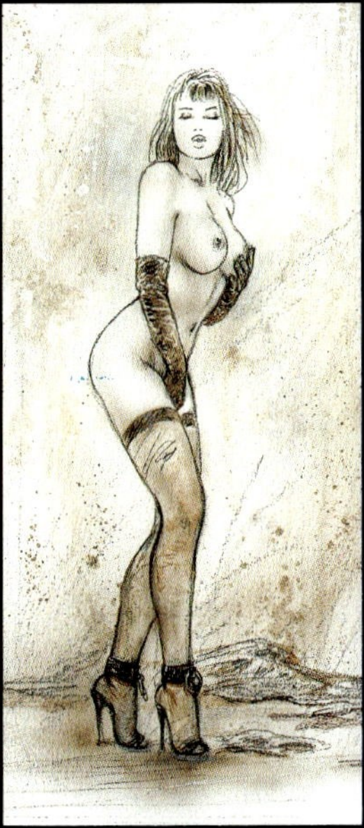

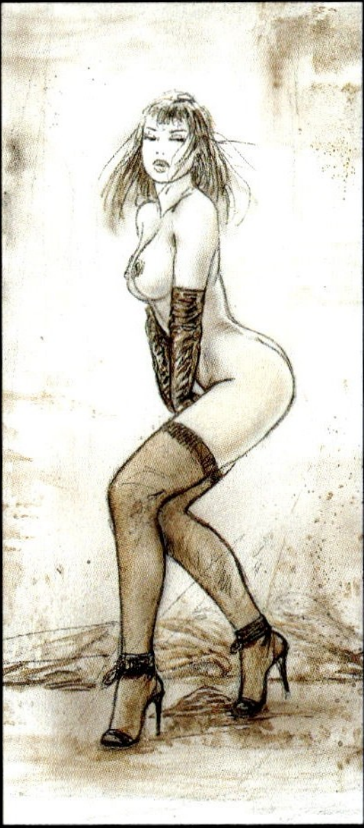

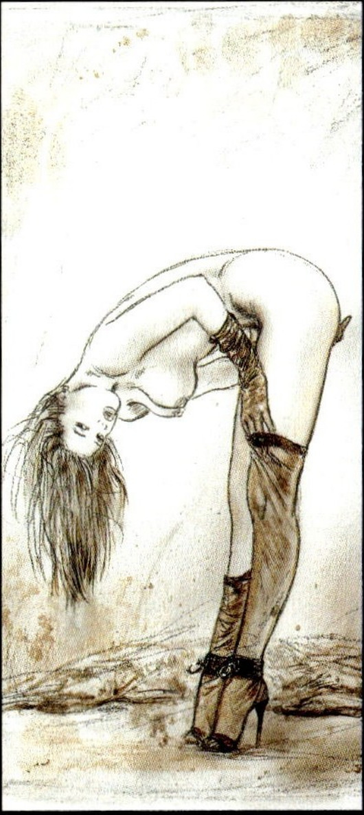

ACT II: THE SPOTLIGHT

Once again, the theatre curtain opens up with the second act, and the second actor appears on the stage. The action is set up. The spectators continue to easily float above their chairs, and if we let ourselves be carried, we'll be able to imagine the place, we'll be able to live the history that's represented.

Shreddings
1998 (32x42 cm.)

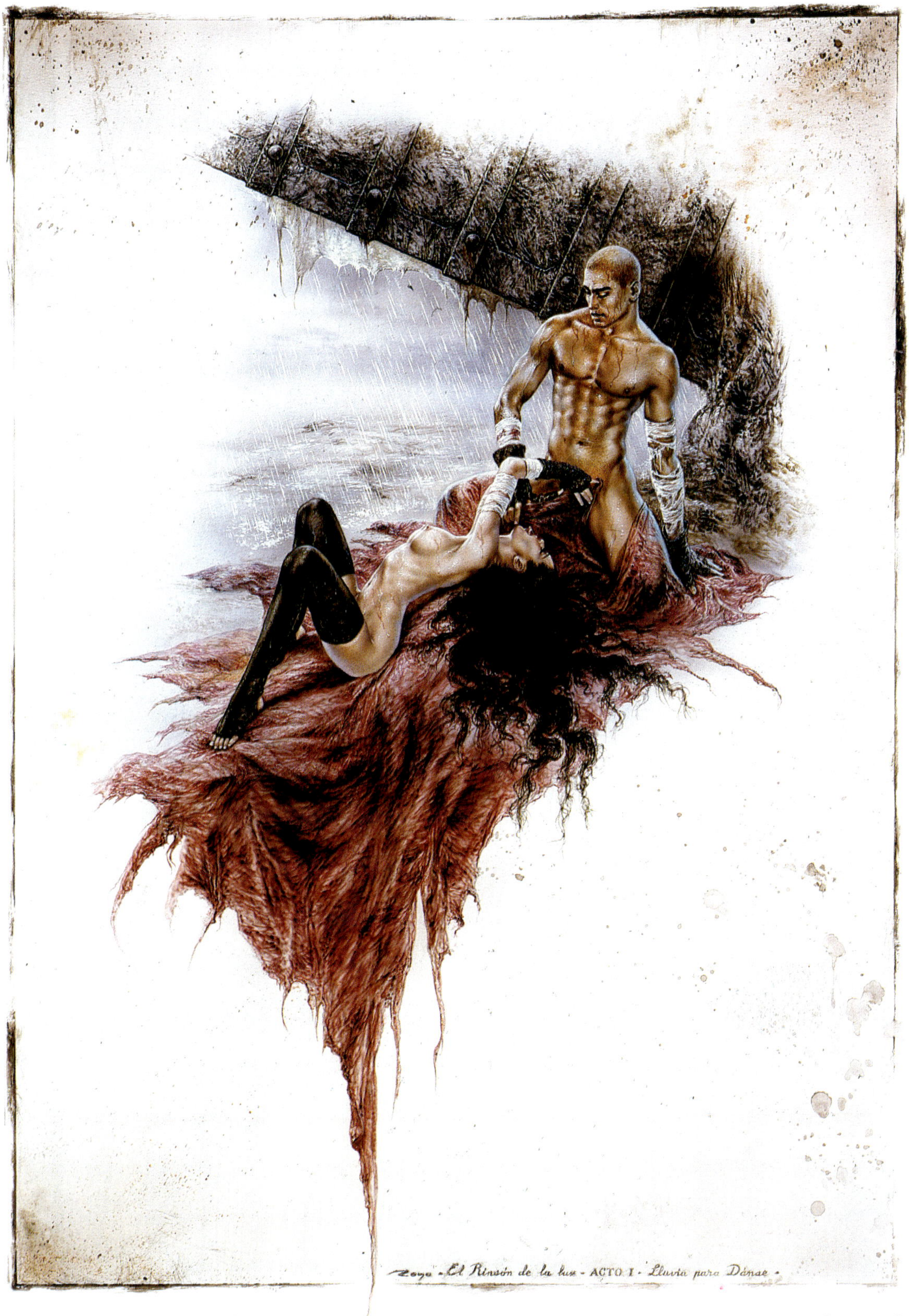
Royo - El Rinsón de la luz - ACTO I - Lluvia para Dánae -

Rain for Danae - 1998 (49x68 cm.)

Under the sheets - 1999 (53x40 cm.)

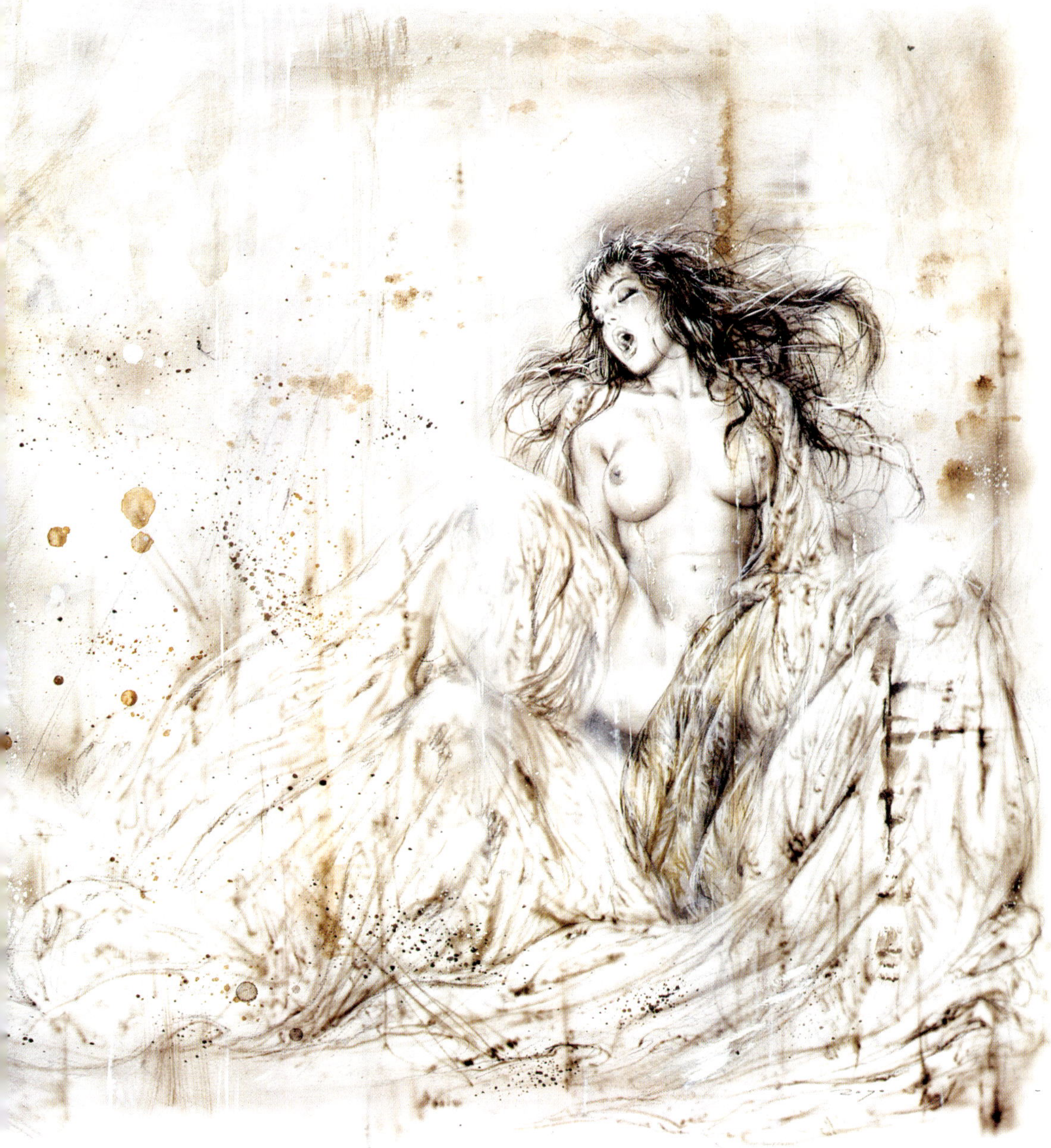

We can submerge ourselves in these infinite sheets and feel the weight of a body that moves rhythmically over us. We can hear some groans, that although don't exist, they form around our heads, pass our ears and submerge inside of us.

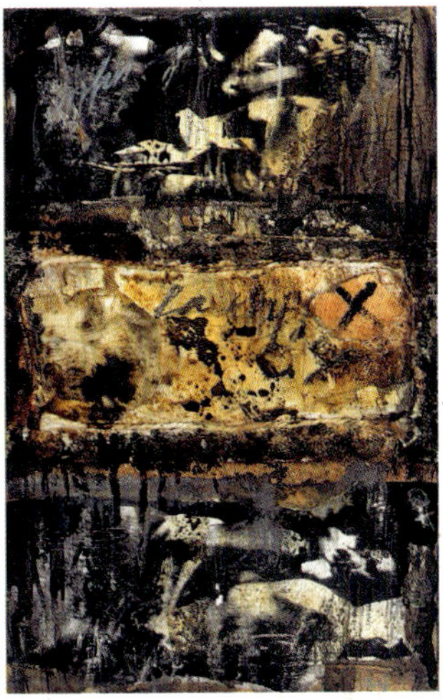

The unfaithful one - 1998 (23,5x35 cm.)
Rómulo Royo

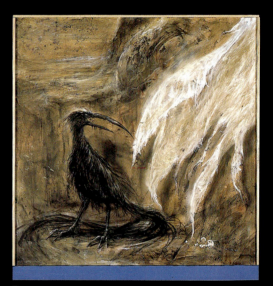

The penultimate voyage - 1998 (445x215 cm.)

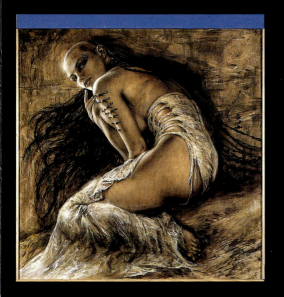

ACT III: MUD ON THE RUGS

I don't know if it's time to raise the curtain or if the third act is supposed to be like a wide open window, where everything is dirty and attractive at the same time, where pain is mistaken for pleasure, where nobody finds or knows the unit of measurement, everyone just utilizes their own. And when the wind blows and the air is filled with particles, some of this dust drops on our shoulders.

Vein hollow - 1998 (20x23 cm.) Rómulo Royo

In the imagination scene, the horizon is able to be so far away that it can disappear. The performers should be left to quickly recite their dialogue so that the curtain can quickly drop before we are flooded with the feeling of sickness.

The daisy - 1998 (33x49 cm.)

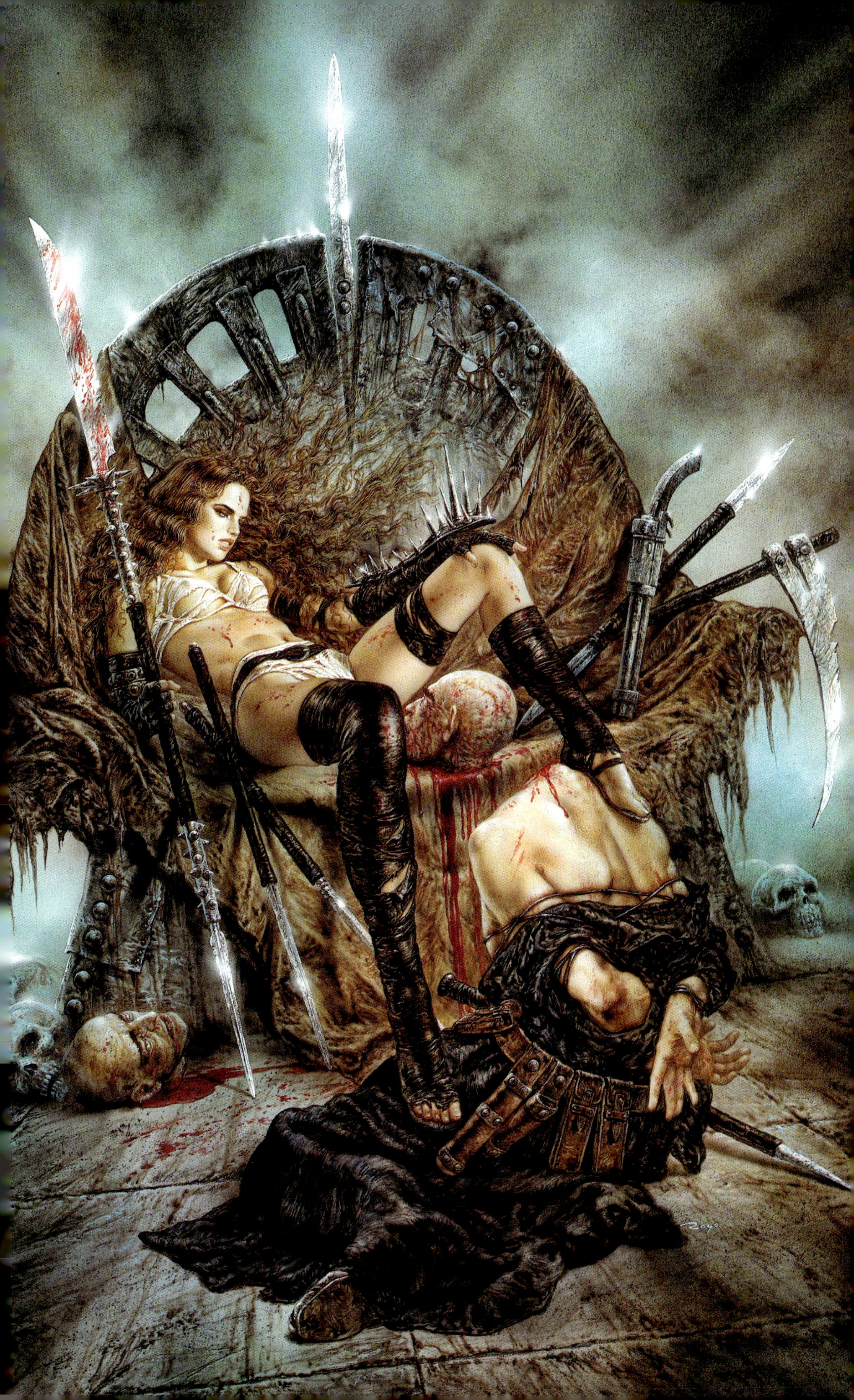

Tangent - 1999 (25,5x40 cm.)

ACT IV: THE ROOM OF MIRRORS

The fourth act of this play doesn't express much to all the spectators. It's the room full of mirrors where you can get yourself lost or you can forget to spend the eighth grave of the infinity. It is the broken rule.

In the garden
1991 (53,5x32,5 cm.)

The performers often show up with masks like in the Greek theatre. The atmosphere is filled with a large unknown that in its zigzagging gives off all the aromas of desire.

A wig to live 1999 (49x36,5 cm.)

Second circle - 1998 (32x49 cm.)

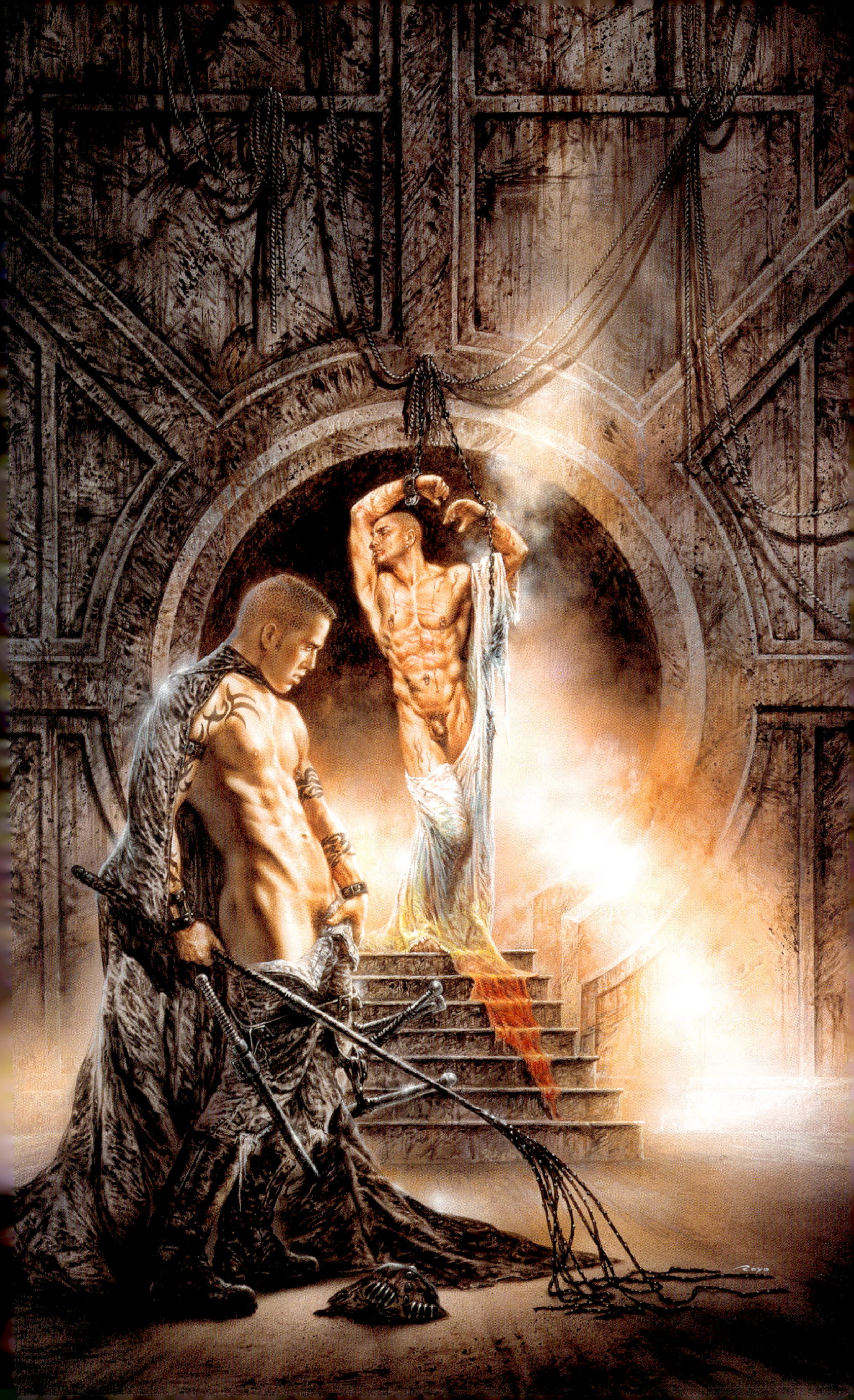
Royo

Memories - 1999 (89x115 cm.) Rómulo Royo

ACT V: CLOSING THE CIRCLE

And in the last act, there is only provocation, self-satisfaction. All the performers of this satire/drama have been vanishing, the play can't make us forget that we still aren't satisfied. The leading actress waits in vain for the entrance of a new actor, but its time to close the circle.

The final hour and the last actor. All that is left is the monologue and her epilogue. The hand conceals what is lost between the creases and the search for the place.

Blind woman's buff
1999 (23,5x41 cm.)

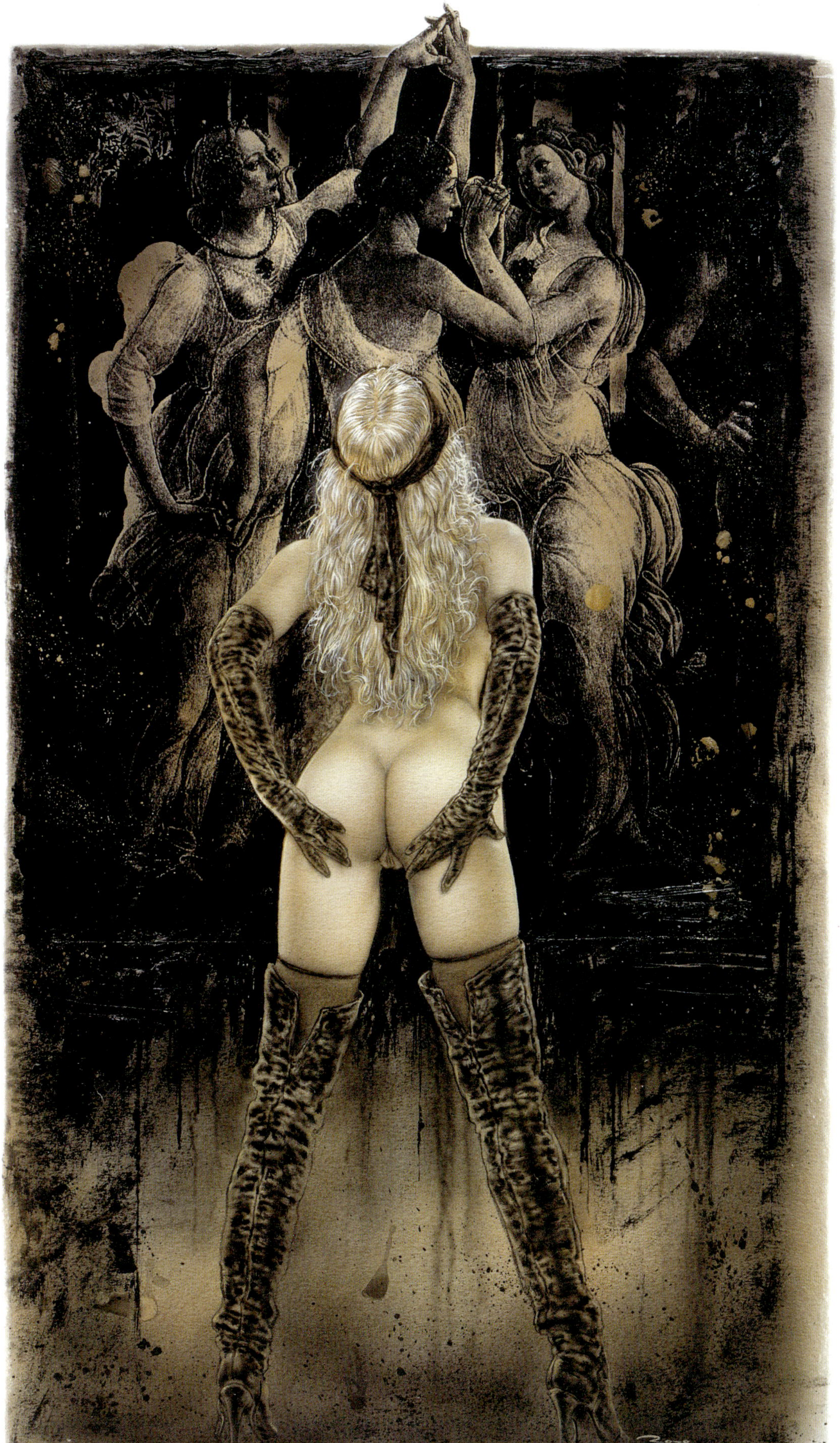

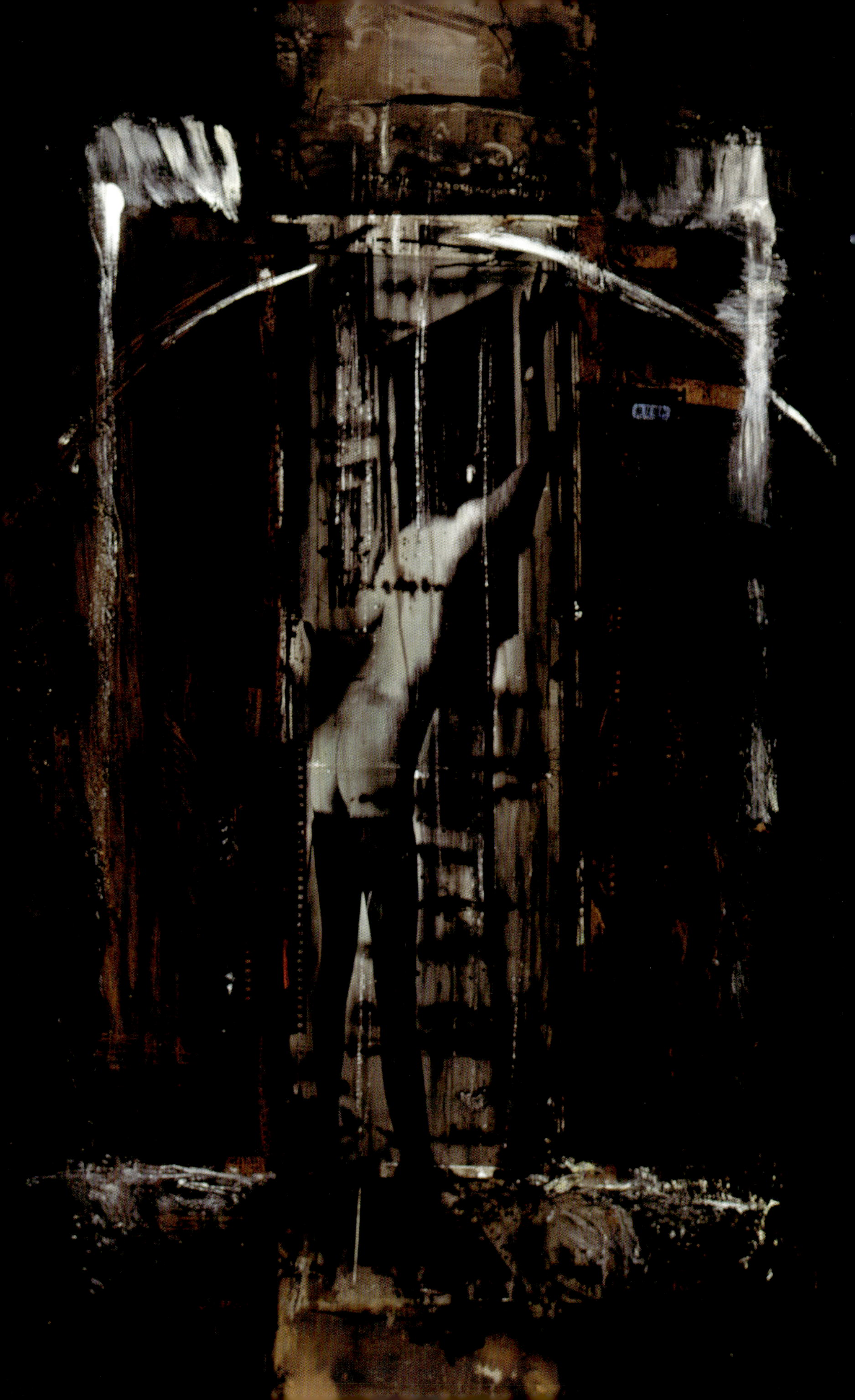

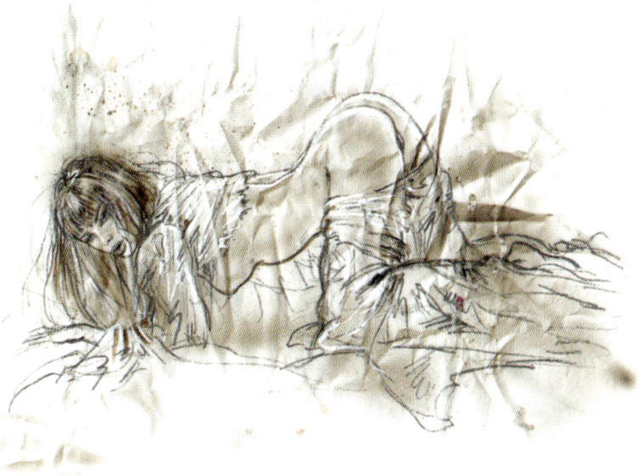

The cyclical and circular act finally closes the curtains, fills our fingers with liquids and forces us to quickly close this book.

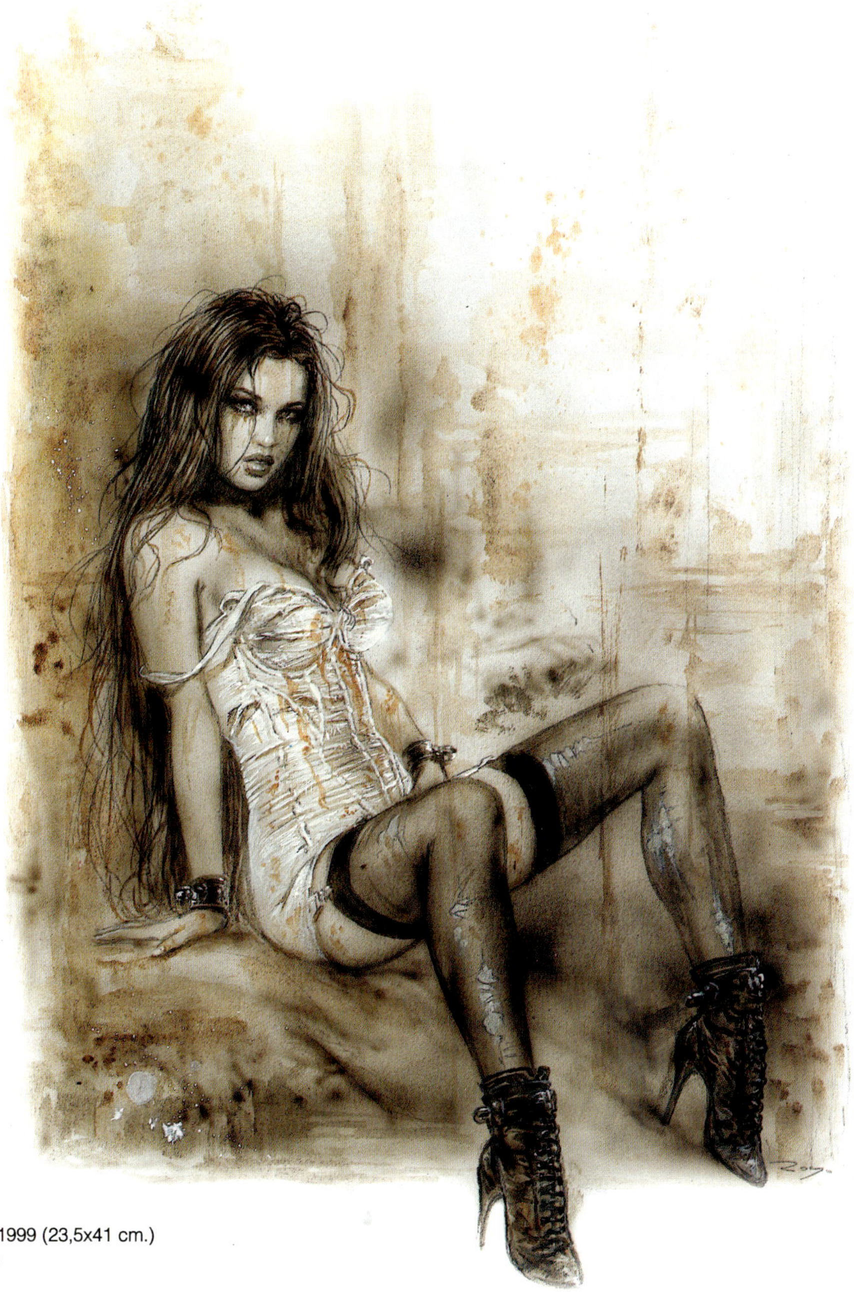

Alone - 1999 (25,5x36,5 cm.)

Case 4668 - 1999 (23,5x41 cm.)
Rómulo Royo

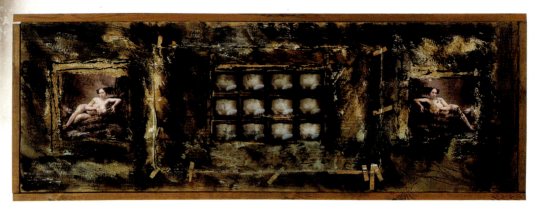

Digital - 1997 (132x44 cm.) Rómulo Royo

Prohibited (35x57 cm.)

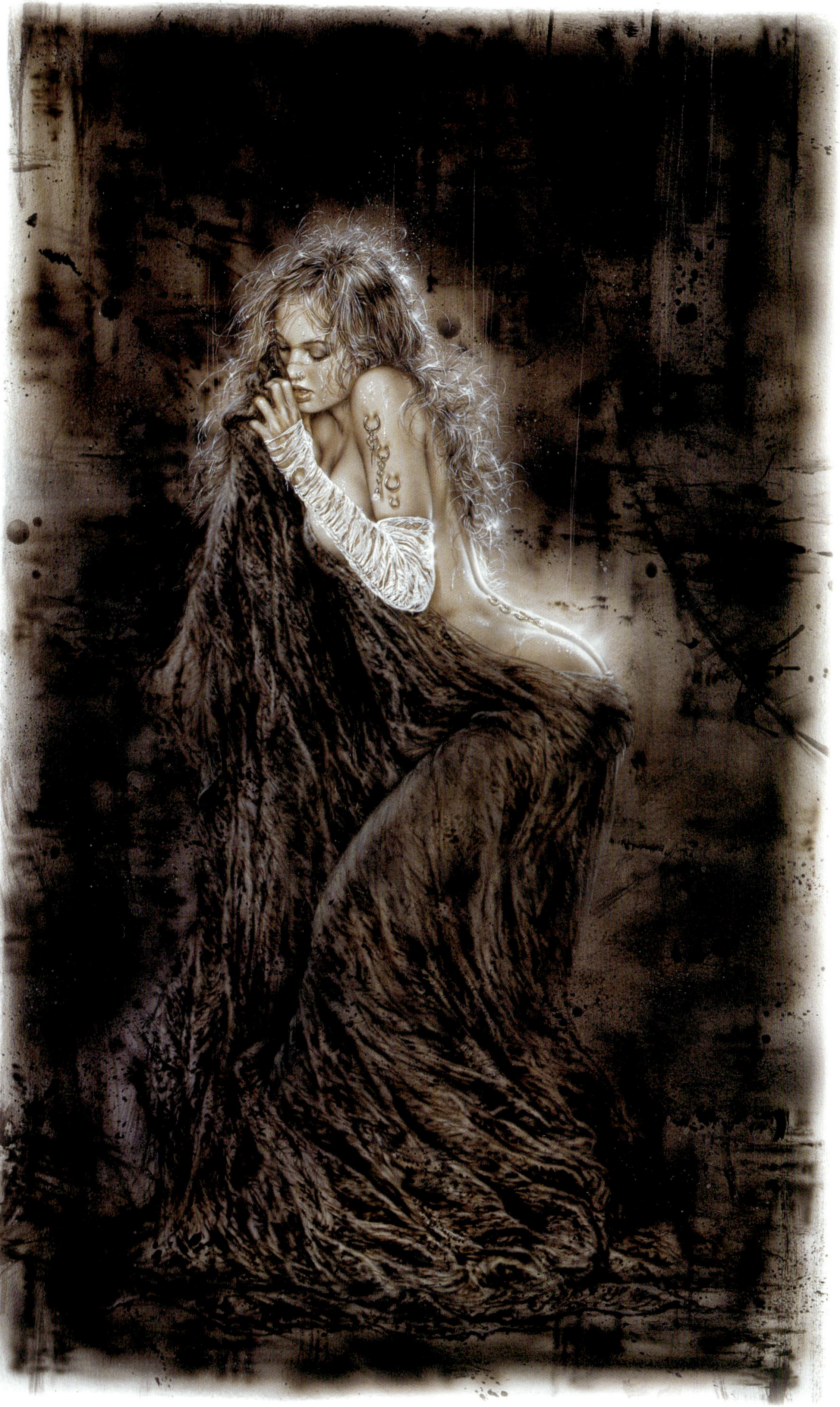

LUIS ROYO BIBLIOGRAPHY

ILLUSTRATED BOOKS

WOMEN

MALEFIC

SECRETS

III MILLENNIUM

DREAMS

PROHIBITED BOOK

PUUF OF DEVILS
(In preparation)

TRADING CARD COLLECTIONS

FROM FANTASY TO REALITY

FORBIDDEN UNIVERSE

THE BEST OF ROYO

SECRETS

MILLENNIUM

PORTFOLIOS

WARM WINDS

III MILLENNIUM

OTHERS

THE BLACK TAROT
Pack of 78 tarot cards

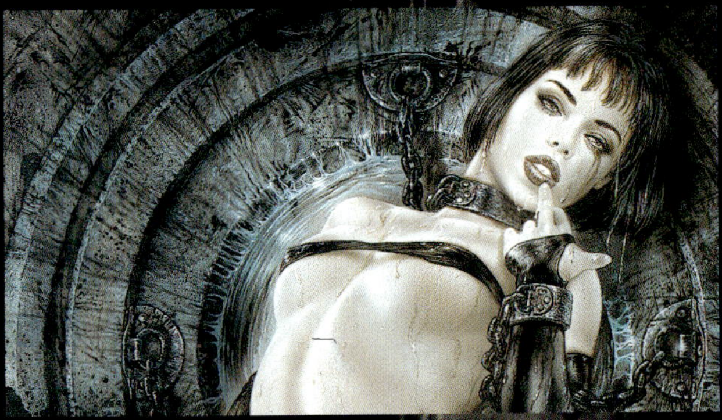

The perversion continues in
PROHIBITED 2.
Coming soon.